FOR MY SON RICHARD,
with all the love in the world

PARENTS' MAGAZINE PRESS, INC.
52 Vanderbilt Ave., New York 17, N. Y.

THE
MOUSE
AND THE
LION

by Eve Titus

illustrated by Leonard Weisgard

There was once a mouse
who wished to see the world of people.

So he said farewell
to his friends in the fields,
and set out in search of a city.

There was once a lion
who also wished to see the world of people.

So he said farewell
to his friends in the forest,
and set out in search of a city.

Along a winding, rambling road they walked—
first the mouse,
and then, a few miles behind him,
the lion.

Neither knew of the other,
nor that they shared the selfsame wish—
to visit the world of people.

Now it chanced that a kind fairy flew by,
and looked down at the little mouse.

Where he was going was no secret
to one with magic powers.

Sadly she said to herself, "Oh, the pity of it!
This poor mouse will be filled with fear
at his first sight of people.
To him they will appear as great giants,
with voices that thunder like mighty waterfalls!
And what if he should be stepped upon by mistake?"

Tears rushed to her eyes at the dreadful thought.
"How can I help this helpless mouse?"
she asked herself, and the answer came at once.

Waving her wand in the air, she whispered,
*"In the eyes of all people who look upon him,
this mouse will appear larger than the largest lion!"*

And away the fairy flew, to meet her godmother.

But a bit farther along, she spied the lion.

Where *he* was going was no secret to her, either.

Sadly she said to herself, "Oh, the pity of it!
Those poor people will be filled with fear
at their first sight of an uncaged lion.
To them he will appear terrifying,
with his fierce, ferocious roar,
and his strong, sharp claws,
even though he means no harm to anyone."

Tears rushed to her eyes at the terrible thought.
"How can I help these helpless people?"
she asked herself, and the answer came at once.

Waving her wand in the air, she whispered,
*"In the eyes of all people who look upon him,
this lion will appear smaller than the smallest mouse!"*

Then her eyes twinkled. "There'll be many a mixup today!"

And away the fairy flew—right out of this book!

Meanwhile, the mouse had halted before a country school.

Two boys with their backs to him were in the yard,
banging blackboard erasers together.

Eager to get a good look at these large creatures,
he crept close, and breathed in some of the chalkdust.

I mustn't, I simply *mustn't* sneeze, he told himself.
But his nose wiggled, his whiskers waggled,
and out came AH— AH— AH— CHOO!

Startled, the two boys turned around,
and stared straight into the eyes
of what *seemed* to be the World's Most Enormous Mouse!

They dropped the erasers, and ran inside screaming,
"MOUSE MONSTER! MOUSE MONSTER!
EVERYBODY HIDE!"

The mouse was puzzled. "Well! People are peculiar.
Why should such giants flee from a midget like myself?
Are these the brave, clever creatures
of whom we mice have heard such fine tales?
Still, it may be that not all are cowards—
I shall seek people who are more like people."

And he scurried out of the schoolyard.

When the boys began screaming,
everyone in school ran to the windows,
expecting to see some weird monster.

Naturally, there was none in sight.

The two boys were told to stop fibbing, to skip recess,
and to write this sentence five hundred times:
A MOUSE IS NOT A MONSTER.

Two by two, the other students marched outside,
wearing their brightest smiles,
for recess is always a favorite subject.

Soon they were all busy playing—
some walked, some ran,
some skipped, some hopped,
some jumped, some fell,
and some actually stood still.

IT WAS JUST ABOUT THEN ...

...THAT THE LION ARRIVED!

Edging up to the iron fence, he said, "At last—people!
Rather smaller than I'd expected, but pleasant enough.
Full of energy, too—they scarcely ever stop moving.
But why on earth do they walk on their hind legs?
Walking on all four would be far more sensible.
And isn't it time they took notice of *me*, a mighty lion?
I shall try to attract their attention."

Deciding that his regular roar
would frighten them much too much,
he poked his nose through the bars
and gave a low little ghost of a growl.

It attracted attention, all right,
but not the kind he'd had in mind!

A first-grade girl bent down and said,
"Girls, girls! Look at the teeny weeny lion!"

"Isn't he precious!" said another. "The little doll!
I'd like to do his hair up in curlers,
and dress him in pink pajamas and pink hairbows,
and wheel him around in my best doll carriage!"

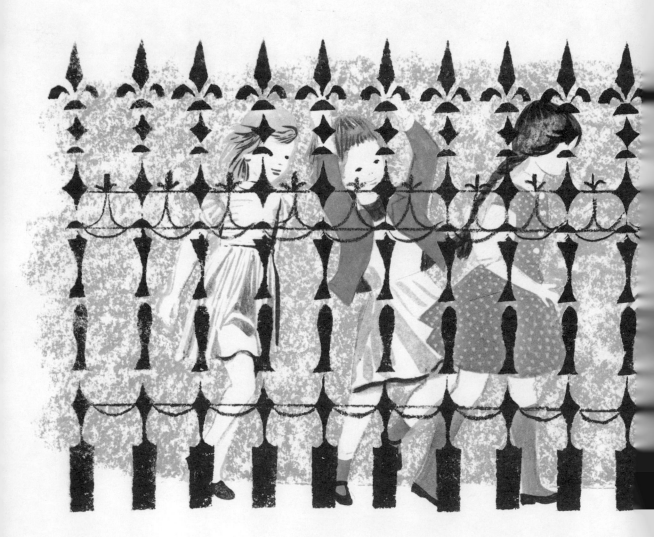

The first girl stamped her foot. "*I* found him!
He'll use *my* doll's curlers, and *my* doll's clothes,
and live in *my* doll house! So there!"

I must be imagining things, thought the lion.
My forest animals quake and shake if I so much as hiccup—
don't these people recognize the King of Beasts?
I'll roar my loudest roar,
and see them scatter like leaves in an autumn wind!

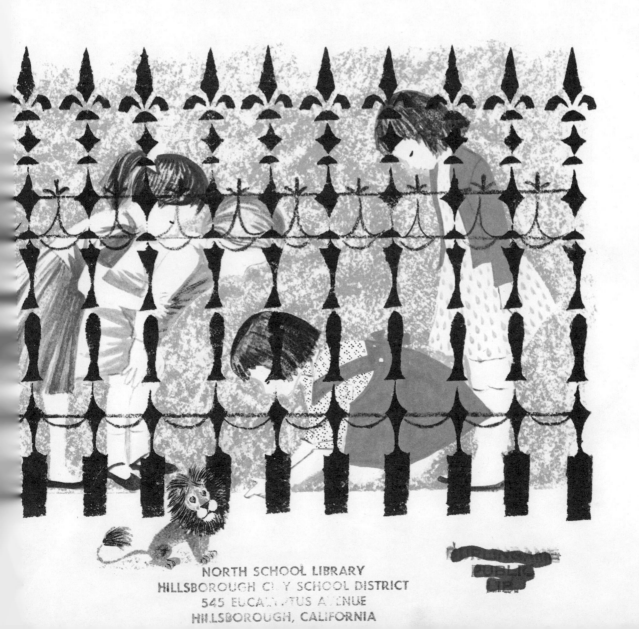

But the girls giggled when he roared, and one said,
"Such a loud, ugly sound for such a sweet pet—
how I wish I could teach him to purr!"

Just then the whistle blew—recess was over.

"I'll put him in my pocket," said the first girl,
and reached between the bars, but he backed away.

With his heart pounding like a hundred hammers,
the lion raced toward the road!

These creatures couldn't be people, he told himself.
No doubt they were beings from another planet—
hadn't his father said that all people feared lions?

So once again he followed the winding, rambling road.

The mouse, meanwhile, was further along the road,
admiring a magnificent white marble building—
the Museum of Natural History.

He knew nothing of museums, but it looked so elegant
that he entered one of the mouseholes in the rear.

There, a mouse he met thought he sought food,
and invited him to luncheon at the museum restaurant.

Politely he refused, explaining why he had come.

"So you want to see people," said the other.
"How dull. Still, each to his own taste.
Plenty of people come here, but for your real reward,
try the second floor—BIG CATS!
Tigers, leopards, and others, looking *so* alive—
but all as dead as can be! What a beautiful sight!"

"Wouldn't miss it for the world!" said the visitor,
and dashed upstairs at once.

How truly his new friend had spoken!
He had a fine view of a great hall—
at its other end, behind a wall of glass,
were several enormous cats.

There they stood, as large as life,
unable to lift a paw!

Tears of joy streamed down his cheeks.
"How lifelike, how very lifelike!" he exclaimed.

"How very lifelike!" said a voice in his ear.

He nodded, thinking that his friend had followed,
but then he noticed two people staring at him.

Trembling to the tip of his tail, he stood there.

"It's a new exhibit," said one. "Do you suppose
there were once mouse monsters on earth?"

Could it be that they meant *him?* Ridiculous!
Yet he did not dare to move—they were watching.

To make matters worse,
some leftover chalkdust began to tickle his nose.

He put his paws over his mouth, but it was no use—
his head bobbled back and forth in a funny way,
and out slipped not one, not two,
but—*three sneezes!*

"EE-EE-EE-YOW! IT'S ALIVE! MOUSE MONSTER!
RUN FOR YOUR LIVES!"

What a hustle! What a bustle!
What a hurry! What a flurry!
It was like a five-alarm fire—
people ran this way and that way,
and that way and this way!

They scrambled for the doors,
they even climbed out of the windows,
trying to escape from what they believed to be
the World's Largest Mouse!

The hall was soon empty of people.

The mouse made a face. "Enough is enough!
I've had my fill of these 'fraidycats.
It's time to go home."

And down the nearest mousehole he dashed,
mumbling under his breath,
"If those are people, then I'm glad I'm a mouse!"

Later, the lion approached the deserted building,
and was also impressed by its beauty.

What he knew about natural history museums
could be written on the head of a pin, but he entered.

Inside, he saw steps curving gracefully upward.
A stairway fit for a king, thought he,
and took the white marble steps two at a time.

Alas for the lion—the steps led to the second floor!

First to meet his eyes was an old enemy,
a tiger with whom he had fought many battles,
and who had vanished mysteriously some time ago.

Now the tiger was a helpless prisoner,
standing motionless behind a wall of glass,
one paw poised in mid-air.
The wall was so high and so thick
that it had no beginning or ending.

The lion grew greatly afraid—
if this was what people did to tigers,
what terrible thing would they do to lions?

He must leave at once,
this very minute, this very second,
before it was too late!

And he bounded down the stairway,
six steps at a time!

But before he reached the door, a museum guard entered!

The lion cowered and cringed, wondering where to hide.

"I can't believe my eyes," said the guard.
"I've never seen so small a lion.
Dr. Leonardo, our lion specialist, will be delighted!
I'll place the lion on his desk, in a little cage."

That was all the lion needed to hear!
Tucking his tail between his legs,
he whizzed out and away!

On the road he fairly leaped along,
his huge paws raising clouds of dust!

AND AS LUCK WOULD HAVE IT...

...his paw struck something soft—the mouse!

The lion picked him up and dusted him off, saying,
"Forgive me! I'd never dream of hurting a mouse,
nor would any lion or lioness I know.
We well remember that long-ago time
when one of yours saved the life of one of ours."

"My fault," said the mouse. "Wasn't watching the road.
I'm overtired—just visited the world of people."

"YOU, TOO?" asked the lion. "What happened?"

The mouse shrugged. "You wouldn't believe it.
Imagine—they were afraid of ME, a mere mouse!"

"Afraid of YOU?" the lion replied. "Impossible!
They're as brave as lions, even braver!"

"Come now," said the surprised mouse.
"You're joking, aren't you?"

The lion thought—why should I be ridiculed,
or run the risk of losing my throne?
None must know how I fared in the world of people!

So he said quickly, "Of course I was joking!
Let me give you a lift home, little mouse,
but first tell me this—do you fear me?"

"Who doesn't?" replied the mouse. "Aren't you our king,
the bravest, strongest, wisest animal in the world?"

"Climb aboard!" commanded the king, smiling.

The lion's long strides shortened the way
to the end of the winding, rambling road.

The mouse was met by friends who clapped and cheered
to see him sliding down the lion's tail!

He lived happily thereafter,
and of one thing you may be sure—
never again did he visit the world of people.

The lion hurried homeward
through the fields.

At the edge of the forest
were animals
from far and near,
gathered there
to give the lion
a truly royal welcome,
as was proper and fitting
for the King of Beasts.

He lived happily thereafter,
and of another thing
you may be sure—
never again
did he visit
the world of people.